This igloo book

belongs to:

....

Published in 2018
by Igloo Books Ltd
Cottage Farm
Sywell
NN6 0BJ
www.igloobooks.com

GOL002 0718
6 8 10 9 7 5
ISBN: 978-1-78197-296-0

Printed and manufactured in China

THE BUNGED UP TRUNK

igloobooks

There was to be a concert in the jungle.
The animals were getting prepared.
All except a little elephant,
who was feeling very **scared.**

Elephant was worried. He was filled up with doubt.
"I've never trumpeted before," he said.

"What if nothing comes out?"

"I'll eat some sticky buns," said Elephant.
"I'll have a good **chew.**
They'll make me feel better.
Then I'll know what to do."

Elephant was busy **chewing,** trying to figure things out.
When suddenly, behind him, there was a very **loud** shout.

"Hello, Elephant!"

roared Tiger. He made Elephant jump and
suck a whole sticky bun,
right up his trunk!

Elephant **waggled** his trunk.
He **waved** it about.

But the bun
wouldn't
budge.

It just **wouldn't** come out.

"Oh, dear," said Tiger.
"You've got a
bun-shaped bump,
that's stopping your trumpet
coming out of your trunk!"

Tiger didn't know whether he
should **laugh** or **cry**.
Then, suddenly, he noticed Cheetah running by.

"Elephant has got a **bunged up trunk!"** cried Cheetah, whizzing past.

He told everyone at the waterhole. The news was spreading fast.

Elephant tried, he **puffed** and **blew.**
He did everything an elephant could do.

Today he was simply out of luck.
"Let's face it," said Frog.
"Your trumpet is stuck."

"Help him!" cried Hippo. "The concert's tonight."
The animals all muttered. They knew Hippo was right.

"Tickle him!" said Monkey.
"That should do the trick.
Come on, everyone,
get tickling, **quick!**"

Elephant **chuckled** and **giggled**. He **laughed** until he cried.
But the bun wouldn't move, no matter how **hard** he tried.

So, Elephant **sucked** up some water and gave a great

SNORT!

Whoosh! it rushed out,
but the bun was still caught.

"Urgh!" cried the animals.

They were all **dripping** wet
and that stubborn sticky bun hadn't come out yet.
"Hurry up!" cried Hippo. "We've got to work faster.
Otherwise the concert will be a **disaster!"**.

They **jiggled** and **wobbled,** but soon it was clear.
The stuck, sticky bun was not going to appear.

Elephant was **exhausted**. He lay **sprawled** on the floor.
"Let the bun stay," he moaned. "I can't take any more.
I've got no more go. I'm all out of puff.

I'm afraid, my good friends, I've just had enough."

At first Elephant felt **upset,** he felt **silly** and **sad.**

But then, he felt **angry.** He got **red-faced** and **mad.**

The **stuck** bun **shot out** and **whooshed** overhead.
"I knew making him angry would work!" Tiger said.

Elephant got ready for the concert. He couldn't wait to go.
His trumpet was **tremendous,** he was
the **star** of the show.

Elephant was **thrilled** and had so much more fun
because at last he was rid of the **stuck, sticky bun!**